BATMAN & ROBIN ADVENTURES

CATWOMAN'S PURRFECT PLOT

BY SARAH HINES STEPHENS

ILLUSTRATED BY
LUCIANO VECCHIO

BATMAN CREATED BY BOB KANE
WITH BILL FINGER

CONTENTS

CHAPTER 1

CATNIP

"And if you will follow me into the next room . . ." The Gotham City Art Museum guide held her hand over her head. She led a group of Brentwood Academy students further into the Egyptian exhibit.

Tim Drake lingered at the back of the group. He was hoping to take a closer look at some of the ancient artefacts. The touring exhibition had only just opened in Gotham City, and many of the priceless pieces were on display for the first time. It was thrilling to see the rare relics up close! And one item in particular had caught Tim's attention.

When the crowd cleared, Tim moved closer to a large glass case and bent down to peer inside the locked display. Inside was an ancient-Egyptian necklace honouring the Egyptian god, Atum-Ra. The wide necklace was made of layered gold beads. It was large enough to cover most of a person's chest, from shoulder to shoulder. And it had been embellished with precious gems that enhanced the necklace's golden glow. A large cat pendant gleamed at the centre of the necklace.

Something about the cat pendant made the hair on the back of Tim's neck stand on end. He read the sign beside the necklace, letting the words sink in. Then he sucked in his breath! If what the sign said was true –

"Careful. Don't fog up the glass," a woman's voice behind him teased.

Tim whirled around. But before he could see who had spoken he felt his phone vibrate in his pocket. Tim took out his phone and checked the screen. A call was coming in from his mentor, Bruce Wayne.

Tim wasn't allowed to answer his phone at school, even if he was on a school trip. But he always found a way to answer Bruce's calls. After all, Bruce Wayne was not just anybody. He was the head of Wayne Enterprises and one of Gotham City's richest, smartest and most generous citizens.

And Bruce Wayne had a secret: he was Batman! Just the person Tim wanted to talk to.

"Bruce! You won't believe what I've just seen. There's a new exhibit at –" Tim was so excited he began talking at once, forgetting that Bruce had called *him*.

"Tim. Listen to me," Bruce cut him off. "I need you to meet Commissioner Gordon and me by the Bat-Signal on the roof of the police station. Come as quickly as you can!"

Bruce hung up before Tim could get another word out. This had to be urgent! Quickly, the boy stashed his phone and looked around. His classmates had moved to another room with the tour guide.

Nobody noticed when Tim made a dash for the exit.

* * *

On the roof of the police station, Batman and the commissioner were waiting. Tim arrived out of breath. He'd taken a moment to change into his alter ego: Robin, the Boy Wonder. Bruce Wayne wasn't the only person in Gotham City with a secret identity!

"Batman, you won't believe the –"

Robin stopped himself mid-sentence when he noticed the look in Batman's eyes. He could read the expression clearly, even behind a mask. Now was not the time.

Robin clamped his mouth shut. He turned to face the man wearing an overcoat beside the Dark Knight, giving the commissioner his full attention.

"Commissioner Gordon, how can we help?" Robin asked.

Batman answered for him. "The commissioner was just telling me that Catwoman has been spotted prowling around the city at night."

Robin nodded, waiting to hear more about Catwoman's whereabouts. There was nothing unusual about her being out at night.

"I know what you're thinking, Robin," Batman continued. "Cats are nocturnal."

"And Catwoman has always been more active at night," Robin agreed.

"Yes, but this is something different," Batman continued. "The commissioner thinks she's working on a plan. She's been seen frequently at Gotham Arena, where they're getting ready for a cat show."

"That's right." Commissioner Gordon nodded. "Gotham City is hosting the International Cat Enthusiasts show. The cat competition begins tomorrow, but the cats and their handlers have already arrived."

Robin frowned. He was still confused. Yes, Catwoman loved cats, but why would the notorious cat burglar care about a pet show? There was hardly anything to be gained from stealing pets.

"The reigning cat champion, Persian Purrfection, will be among the competing cats," Gordon continued. "Purrfection is considered to be a near flawless specimen of her breed. She is worth a lot of money."

"But Catwoman would never *sell* a cat," Robin said. "She thinks cats should be free!"

As far as Robin could tell, if Catwoman had her way the whole world would be overrun with cats. Or maybe cats would simply run it!

"The prize cat is just part of it, Robin," Batman continued. "Persian Purrfection wears the ICE crown."

"The ICE crown?"

"It's a collar created by the International Cat Enthusiasts and given to the Best in Show," said Commissioner Gordon.

"The winner wears it for one year," Batman explained. "Then brings it back to either win it again or pass it to the next Best in Show."

"How valuable could a cat collar be?" Robin asked, raising one eyebrow.

"It's not just any collar, Robin," Batman replied. "It's encrusted with nine rare feline-cut diamonds. Each gem looks like a sparkling cat's eye. The prize is worth millions of dollars."

Batman found an image of the collar on his mini-computer. He turned it to show the Boy Wonder.

Robin let out a low whistle. *THWOOOO!*

The collar did look pretty spectacular. He could hardly believe that someone would put something that incredible on a cat!

Commissioner Gordon ran his hand through his white hair. He gritted his teeth.

"If something happens to that cat or that collar, it will be an international embarrassment for our city," Gordon said. "It's crucial that we keep them both safe while they are in Gotham City."

"You're absolutely right, Commissioner," Batman said with a nod. "The combination of precious cats *and* precious jewels will be like catnip for Catwoman – too much for her to resist."

Precious cats and precious jewels. Hearing his mentor's words reminded Robin of what he'd been trying to say earlier. His eyes widened behind his mask.

"Exactly!" Robin exclaimed. "That's what I've been –"

He started to tell the Dark Knight and Commissioner Gordon what he'd been thinking earlier, but he was interrupted.

"That's why I need you two to help guard the Gotham Arena tonight!" Gordon said. "We have to make sure nothing goes wrong before the competition tomorrow."

CRRRRCHT!

Suddenly, Commissioner Gordon's police radio crackled to life. He reached for it.

"I've already pulled half of the force and most of the city's armed guards to help." The police commissioner put the radio to his ear. "But Catwoman is tricky. You never know when she's going to pounce!" he added.

Batman gave a slight nod. Nobody knew better than he did how sneaky Catwoman could be.

But there was something else troubling the Dark Knight. He was picking up distress signals coming from the other side of the city. With the help of the audio processor and high-gain antenna housed in the pointed ears of his cowl, he could detect the sound of a distant alarm – a large one.

At the same time that Batman was picking up these sounds, the commissioner was getting bad news over the radio. The two were connected, and Batman knew what the head of the Gotham City Police Department was going to say even before he said it.

"There's a security breach at the arena!" the commissioner exclaimed, putting down his radio.

"Catwoman's already got the jump on us!" Batman announced, scowling. "Come on, Robin. We haven't a moment to lose."

CHAPTER 2

BATS IN A CAVE

Batman and Robin raced to the Batmobile and leaped inside. The sun started to set as they sped across the city. Buckled into the passenger seat, Robin tried again to tell Batman about what he had seen at the art museum. "Batman, there's something in the new exhibit that I –"

"No time for that now, Robin," Batman said, silencing the Boy Wonder. The Dark Knight steered smoothly around traffic and into the arena car park. "We need to focus on the job at hand."

Robin looked out of the window. The closed arena was next to the huge Knights football stadium. The two buildings shared a massive car park. The space around the smaller arena was full of police and uniformed guards. They were all milling around, looking up at the arena and scratching their heads. Some of them were covering their ears to block out the noisy alarm that was still sounding.

WEE-OO! WEE-OO! WEE-OO!

Batman and Robin leaped from their vehicle. They spotted the chief of police standing by the closed arena entrance and hurried over to get the latest news.

"What's going on?" Batman asked.

"We rigged the ICE collar to activate an alarm and seal all of the entrances and exits if it was unclasped," the chief shouted.

"Someone must have taken it off of the cat!" exclaimed Robin.

"The good news is that the alarm worked," continued the chief. "The arena is completely locked down. There is no way the thief can get out. The bad news is, we hadn't finished programming the alarm. We haven't set the deactivation code. So there's no way anybody can get in, either!"

"That's what you think." Batman jogged away from the arena with Robin on his heels. He headed towards the football stadium on the other side of the car park.

Robin didn't question his partner's actions very often. He knew that Batman was familiar with the plans for Knights Stadium. Bruce Wayne had funded the city project. He had even approved the plans, back when the stadium was being built.

As the caped pair jogged towards the larger building, Batman scanned the outside walls. When they were close enough he fired his cement-penetrating grapnel, securing a jump line. Robin followed suit and fired his own grapnel gun.

THWIP!

An ultra-thin wire pulled each hero to the top of the stadium.

"What are we doing up here?" Robin asked when they'd regained their footing.

"Looking for a fast way down," Batman answered.

The Caped Crusader leaped off the wall. He touched down briefly in each seating section before rushing forward and jumping off of the balcony to get to the tier below. Like a flying squirrel, he glided through the air and then landed without a stumble.

Robin followed as quickly as he could. Thanks to his parkour training, the Boy Wonder could make his way around almost any urban environment with acrobatic ease. He took giant leaps, clearing two rows of seats at a time.

When he reached the guard rail on the edge of the upper deck, he vaulted over the ledge.

WHOOSH!

Robin dropped nearly five metres and banked off a wall to slow his fall. He landed in a tuck on the level below, rolled and was back on his feet in an instant.

The combination of gymnastic skill and martial arts training allowed Robin to move without hesitation. He stayed right on Batman's heels all the way down.

When they reached the pitch, Batman did not slow down. He ran into one of the tunnels that led to the dressing rooms, opened a door in the dim corridor and sprinted down another flight of stairs.

"What are we doing down here?" Robin asked, out of breath. He glanced around the darkened corridor. It looked like a tunnel of some kind – a secret passageway. But it wasn't even in the same building where the potential cat-napping was taking place!

"These maintenance tunnels run under the car park and connect the stadium to the arena," Batman explained. "They were built for maintenance workers, but today they'll be our private entrance."

"Great! Which way should we go?" Robin asked, looking around. The tunnels ran in several directions, like a huge maze.

"This way. Follow me, and stay alert," Batman said. "While we're busy looking for a way in, Catwoman is probably looking for a way out!"

Batman ran ahead, turning right, then left, then right, searching for the best path through the tunnels and up to the arena.

Robin followed, getting more and more disorientated.

"We're like rats in a maze!" he called out in frustration.

"No, Robin." Batman chuckled. "We're like bats in a cave. And we're just about ready to fly."

Batman made one more turn. Robin could not see him, but he heard his feet pounding. The footfalls changed as the Dark Knight climbed a set of stairs.

Robin rounded the corner and looked up. In the dim light he watched as Batman placed a pen-sized bat-grenade beside the handle of a locked door. He retreated several steps and shielded himself and Robin with his cape. There was a small explosion. The door blew open, and the Dynamic Duo emerged into the corridors of the arena.

"These interior doors don't have the same locking mechanisms as the main exits," Batman explained.

Robin covered his ears. The noise of the alarm was even louder inside the arena than it had been in the car park. There was another sound, too – the sound of people panicking! By running towards the echoing screams and cries, Batman and Robin found the cat show. As expected, it was in complete chaos.

The cat owners were panicked, running around unsure of what to do to stop the noise, protect their pets and escape the scene.

"We're here to help," Robin tried to reassure them. It did nothing to stop the madness. The young hero looked around, searching for the cat-napper. She had to be here somewhere, but with everyone rushing around, it was hard to tell.

"Please, everyone, calm down!" Robin shouted. It was useless. Nobody could hear him over the racket.

Robin put his hands up to cover his ears. The noise was downright painful! As well as the alarm and the shouting crowd, the cats were also complaining loudly. Extra loudly.

MMIIAADDWW! MMIIAADDWW!

All around the showroom floor were cages filled with frightened felines. Only one large cage was empty: Persian Purrfection's. Inside the other enclosures, several prize cats yowled and paced back and forth.

"Something's upsetting the cats!" one of the owners shouted to Robin.

"Maybe it's the sound of the alarm," Robin shouted back. Cats are sensitive to loud noises. And this noise was beyond loud!

"It's more than that," the owner yelled. She put her hand up to her own cat's cage. The cat hissed and swiped the air. "Mister Whiskers would never normally behave like this! It has to be more than the noise."

"She's right, Robin," Batman said, putting a gloved hand to his cowl. "My filtration systems are picking up something else in the air. Pheromones."

"Pheromones. I remember those from biology lessons. Aren't they the chemicals an animal releases to affect another animal's behaviour?" Robin asked. With so many cats in one building there were bound to be a few cat chemicals in the air.

"That's exactly right, Robin," Batman replied. "But the levels I'm detecting are far more than the usual amount – even in a gathering of cats this big. Someone must be pumping pheromones into the ventilation system to make the cats behave aggressively."

"Guess whoooo?" a sultry, amplified voice purred from above.

Batman and Robin looked up to see Catwoman perched high up in the commentary box. She was stroking a white fluffy cat. A sparkling bracelet glittered on her wrist.

Robin quickly concluded that the bangle was no bracelet. It was lined with eye-shaped jewels. It was the ICE collar!

Catwoman smirked at the two men in capes as she pushed buttons on the box's control panel. Suddenly the alarms stopped.

The crowd on the floor rubbed their ringing ears and rushed for the exits. Although the alarm had stopped, the doors remained sealed.

"It was so hard to think with all of that noise," Catwoman cooed, stroking Persian Purrfection's white coat. "Luckily, I didn't have to think too much. The alarm is broadcast over the intercom system. So that was easy enough to shut down from here. And you've done the rest of my thinking for me, Batman. I won't even have to blast my way out, thanks to you showing me the 'bat' door!"

Catwoman laughed, delightedly. She loved getting the better of Batman.

"But don't worry, Bats," she added. "I'll make sure I'm the *only* person who gets out."

Robin took a step towards the stairs that led up to the commentary box. But Batman put out his hand to stop him.

The Dark Knight knew Catwoman well. He knew this was just a tease. Catwoman was toying with them the way a real cat played with its prey.

"Looks like it's time for us to say goodnight, Batman. But before I go, there's one more thing I'd like to do . . ."

MROOOOOOOWRRR!

A feline yowl and a cold cackle echoed in the huge space. Then all of the lights in the arena went out.

CLICK! SCREEECH!

Robin heard a metallic click, and the screeching of wire on wire. A shiver ran down his spine.

In the pitch-blackness the cat enthusiasts began to panic and shout. Robin jumped as something brushed past his ankle. Then he felt the hand on his shoulder tighten.

"She's releasing the cats," Batman whispered. "She hates cages."

"But how – ?"

"Don't forget, Robin, that Catwoman isn't the only one who can see in the dark."

"Right!" Robin pulled his night-vision goggles from his Utility Belt and put them on. Angry cats streaked around the arena, swiping at any other cat or person that came close and looking for places to hide.

Cat owners fumbled in the dark for phones and torches. Then Robin saw what Batman was focused on. Catwoman had come down from the box. She was walking calmly among them, holding Persian Purrfection in one hand and setting the hostile cats free with the other.

"There she is." Robin pointed.

"I see her," Batman rumbled.

Without another word the Caped Crusader and the Boy Wonder split up. They wanted to approach Catwoman from two sides, to stop her from reaching the door they had come in through.

"Hold it right there, you crazy cat lady," Robin said when they were both standing fairly close.

Catwoman opened another cage.

YOOOWRRR! FFFFFT!

A crying and hissing Siamese leaped down, unsure of where to go. It arched its back, took two steps sideways, spat at Robin and then streaked away into the shadows.

"You're putting these cats in danger!" Robin said.

Catwoman cackled. "I'm just setting them free, little bird. Cats aren't like you *canaries*. We don't belong in cages!"

"I can think of one cat that belongs behind bars!" Robin shot back. He lunged at Catwoman, but the slinky criminal was quick!

Catwoman sprang up and over Robin's head, twisting in the air to avoid his grasp. She landed on her feet on the other side of him and sprinted towards the door. Robin's outstretched arms closed on air.

"Nice try, Boy Blunder," she called over her shoulder.

But when she turned back, she realized she'd made a terrible mistake. She'd taken her eyes off Batman! The detective dropped down in front of her – blocking her exit.

"Hold it right there," Batman said. He planted his feet and crouched down, ready to spring if Catwoman made any sudden moves. He had the jewel thief right where he wanted her!

"Not a chance," Catwoman shot back. "There's more than one way to free a feline."

Knowing that Batman could see as well as she could, Catwoman threw Persian Purrfection and the ICE collar at his chest. Batman caught the collar and white fluffy cat safely, but Catwoman slipped past him!

"She's getting away!" Robin cried.

He lurched after her and nearly tripped over one of the cat owners who was crawling around trying to find his pet.

"That's okay, Robin. Let her go," Batman said softly. "We've got the prize."

With his goggles on, Robin saw what Batman meant. He was holding Purrfection in one arm and the priceless ICE collar in the other. Gently, Batman clipped the collar around the cat's neck – returning Purrfection's prize to the rightful owner.

"Our work here isn't finished yet, Robin," said Batman. "We need to secure these cats before anyone gets hurt."

The Dark Knight pushed the escape door closed with his boot. Then he snapped up the hissing Siamese and placed him in one of the empty cages. Robin put a yowling tabby in another.

When the lights came back on, several minutes later, Batman and Robin had successfully captured and returned most of the cats.

But something was bothering the Caped Crusader. He seemed irritated as he stroked Persian Purrfection, still cradled in one arm.

"I don't quite understand. Why would Catwoman throw away the things she worked so hard to steal? It doesn't make sense . . ." Batman stopped stroking the cat.

"That's what I've been trying to tell you," Robin said. "I think Catwoman may have her eyes on a bigger prize!"

CHAPTER 3

THE CAT'S MIAOW

Batman stared at Robin. The boy had a cat under each arm and a third yowling feline in his outstretched hands.

"What did you say?" Batman asked.

"I've been trying to tell you," Robin explained as he wrestled the captured cats back into cages. "When I was at the museum this morning, I saw an ancient-Egyptian necklace. I think Catwoman may find it irresistible."

Batman raised an eyebrow as he handed Persian Purrfection back to her owner. He raised a gloved finger and pointed at the sparkling collar.

"But as we can see, Catwoman doesn't find *every* jewel irresistible," the Dark Knight replied. "She gave up this bangle without much of a fight."

"True," Robin agreed. "But I'm not talking about just any jewel. And she may have just wanted us to think she was giving up. The necklace at the museum belonged to Atum-Ra, the Egyptian sun god. Atum had eyes like a cat. He could see in the dark and travelled each year to the underworld in feline form. This god and his necklace are right up Catwoman's alley!"

"Yes, but so was the ICE collar," Batman said. As a detective, he was a natural sceptic.

"But Atum-Ra's necklace was more than cat-themed. It has value beyond money. Atum-Ra is the god that created the nine deities that ruled Earth. He's the god behind the myth of cats having nine lives. And legend has it that anyone who wears Atum-Ra's necklace will be granted nine lives of their own and enjoy untold powers," Robin recounted breathlessly. "For Catwoman, it's the cat's miaow!"

"Well, why didn't you say so?" Batman snatched up two more skittish kitties.

"I tried, but –"

Batman cut Robin off again. The police chief had finally made it to the floor of the arena and quickly approached the heroes.

"Good work, Batman," the chief congratulated him.

Batman gave a small nod, but he knew his work was not finished.

"We saved the cat and the collar," the Dark Knight agreed.

"But Catwoman got away," Robin blurted.

"That's right. I'm afraid you and your team are going to have to round up the rest of these cats on your own, Chief," Batman said, handing his captives over to the chief. "We've got a cat burglar to catch!"

The Dynamic Duo ran out of the arena to the waiting Batmobile and sped back across the city. The streets were eerily quiet. Catwoman's little decoy had tied up most of Gotham City's police officers so that she could carry out her real plot in secret. Sending Batman and Robin on a wild goose chase was just part of her master plan.

Batman exhaled slowly and relaxed his grip on the steering wheel. He did not like to be toyed with. But if Catwoman insisted on playing games, he would simply have to insist on winning.

Up ahead, the Gotham City Art Museum loomed large. They were getting close when Batman quickly steered his stealth vehicle into a darkened alley.

"I just spotted two armed guards at the entrance," he told Robin. "But I get the feeling they're not working for the museum."

"Catwoman's goons," Robin muttered under his breath, understanding instantly.

"Exactly." Batman got out of the Batmobile and gazed up at the rooftops, searching for the right place. As soon as he found it he fired the hook from his grapnel gun. The hook caught on a sturdy ledge.

Robin quickly followed suit, choosing a spot a couple of metres away. Moments later, the crime fighters were pulled up on the attached jump lines to the rooftop.

The museum's skylight glowed a few buildings away. Robin followed Batman's lead as they sped over gables and leaped over giant gaps between buildings. When they landed on the museum roof, Batman put up a gloved hand to slow Robin down. The Boy Wonder knew he was warning him to be as quiet as possible.

Silently they crept over to the skylight and peered down into the gallery below.

All was quiet, as far as they could tell. The museum was closed. The Egyptian exhibit was empty, and it appeared that the alarm had been set. Only a few small spotlights glowed inside the display cases.

"That's the necklace!" Robin whispered excitedly, pointing to the large, elegant necklace at the far end of the room. It was just where he had seen it last. They weren't too late!

Or were they?

Batman pushed Robin's hand down, away from the glass, and pulled him back and out of sight. Beneath them a slinky shape emerged from the shadows – a black shape with pointed ears. Catwoman!

The bewitching burglar crossed the room noiselessly. She twitched her head this way and that, looking all around, stepping closer and closer to the necklace. It drew her gaze and did not let go. Her eyes narrowed. When she was close enough, she bent down and rubbed her face up against the case, like a cat welcoming home her master. She was mesmerized by the beautiful necklace.

With his cowl's enhanced hearing, Batman could hear the woman in black softly croon.

"Here, pretty, pretty, pretty," Catwoman purred. "If you really hold all of the powers people claim, no one will be able to stop me from freeing caged cats . . . stopping cat shows all over the world!" With that she balled her fist and slowly raised it.

Batman placed his hand silently on Robin's shoulder once again, this time to alert him that it was almost time to make their move. Robin nodded. The Dark Knight did not have to say a word.

Catwoman raised her fist and brought it crashing down on the glass, shattering the case! At the same moment, Robin and Batman jumped together, smashing the skylight.

CRAAASH!

The pair of heroes broke through the skylight. They swooped down, and landed in the middle of the room in a shower of broken glass.

SWOOSH!

Catwoman spun around. She reared and bared her teeth. She thought she'd taken care of this meddling pair already. The villain was not happy to have her moment interrupted.

"You!" she snarled, glaring at them both. Her eyes flicked from one crime fighter to the other. "I thought I'd dealt with you."

Catwoman's spine arched as she slowly backed up against the case. Without taking her eyes off of Batman and Robin, she reached through the broken glass and seized the necklace.

"But I'm afraid you're already too late!" the villain spat. Then a sly smile spread across her face. "Or, maybe you're just in time –"

In a single swift movement, Catwoman pulled the collar from the case and fastened it around her own neck.

CLICK!

The instant the golden, jewelled collar was fastened, her eyes widened. "I think . . . yes, I think it's . . ."

Her body began to jerk. She dropped to the ground in a crouch, wracked by spasms.

"It's working!" Catwoman yowled.

Batman and Robin stood frozen. Staring.

"I thought it was just a myth," Batman murmured, unable to trust what he saw happening before his eyes.

On the floor before them, Catwoman appeared to be growing a tail. It grew, stretching and uncurling until it resembled a long leathery whip. Talon-like nails tore out of the ends of her black gloves and boots. They scraped on the marble floor sending up a chilling screech. Catwoman flailed around, grimacing. Then she threw her head back and let out an animal howl.

MRRRROOOOOWR!

When at last the writhing stopped, a low growling gurgle – like a lioness warning away enemies – rumbled in Catwoman's throat. She opened her eyes. They glowed golden, cat-like, and widened in surprise as she took in the changes.

"I wasn't sure this would work," she murmured, running her hand over her tail. "But seeing is believing. Don't you think?"

Catwoman locked eyes with the Boy Wonder. One corner of her mouth tugged up into a leering smile, revealing larger, sharper incisors than she'd had before. She licked her lips and flexed her claws. Every muscle in her body was coiled. She was ready to pounce on her chosen prey. "Or maybe *feeling* is believing. Shall we test it?"

Robin was speechless. He stood stock-still, caught in her intense gaze.

He was a sitting duck.

CHAPTER 4

LET SLEEPING CATS LIE

Grasping her whip-tail in one hand, Catwoman swung it over her head, never taking her glowing eyes off Robin. The Boy Wonder froze like a deer in headlights as the villain walked slowly towards him. Batman circled around to get behind the mad cat. He wasn't sure what this transformed Catwoman was capable of.

"How did you know I was here, Batman?" Catwoman asked, her eyes still locked on Robin. Her tail made whooshing sounds as it sliced the air. "Did a little bird tell you?"

Before Batman could answer, Catwoman brought her tail down with amazing speed. Robin lurched to one side, finally breaking free of Catwoman's spell. But he dodged too late. Her tail sliced through the fabric of his suit, and Robin cried out. *AAAHHH!*

Catwoman cackled. "Oooh, looks like I clipped your wing, Robin," she joked. "Maybe I'm not upset that you two are here after all. It allows me to test my new powers!"

Catwoman flexed her talon-like claws and gazed down at herself, admiring the changes Atum-Ra's jewels had brought about. She ran a hand over her arm, satisfied with the muscles pushing against her fitted suit. She held her hands up so her claws glinted in the dim light. She laughed again. *HAHAHAHA!*

Then Catwoman gathered her whip-tail, winding it around her arm like a pet snake.

"All this and nine lives too. I think I'm going to like being a goddess!"

"Not so fast, Catwoman." Batman positioned himself protectively between the feline villainess and his injured ward. He pointed at the glimmering collar circling Catwoman's throat. "Those jewels don't belong to you. And those powers don't belong to you either."

Catwoman didn't want to hear Batman's thoughts on the subject. She hissed at the Dark Knight, baring her teeth before crouching and coiling her muscles to spring.

"Says who?" she snarled.

The two dark figures faced off, circling each other slowly in the museum hall. Both of them bided their time, waiting to see who would strike first. Then Catwoman suddenly pounced.

With a wicked laugh the villainess leaped high into the air. She aimed her feet at the Caped Crusader's chest and landed a solid double kick.

WHACK! SMAACK!

The kick to the chest sent Batman flying across the room.

WHAMMM!

The Caped Crusader slammed into the wall and slowly slid to the ground. Plaster from the smashed wall rained down on the floor around him.

Gotham City's Dark Knight Detective was stunned. He had faced off against his feline nemesis hundreds of times. She had always been a dangerous opponent, but she was now at least ten times more powerful than she'd ever been before!

Batman was still struggling to get air back into his lungs when Catwoman struck again, this time landing in a crouch on his chest. She leaned in close, so that she and Batman were nearly nose to nose.

Catwoman cocked her head. Then she held up a single claw. Slowly she lowered it until the tip rested on Batman's breastplate. The claw slid easily through the fifteen layers of bulletproof fabric that served as his protection.

Batman did not flinch. Not even when he felt Catwoman's claw reach his skin. With the flick of her wrist Catwoman could pierce his chest. But she did not. She was toying with him . . . again.

A bead of sweat escaped Batman's cowl and trickled down his face as he wracked his brain searching for a way out of this cat trap.

Suddenly a shadow passed over the figures on the floor and a loud crack echoed in the great hall. Robin was up! The Boy Wonder had opened the telescoping bo staff he kept on his belt. He brought it down with all of his strength, aiming for Catwoman's back.

Catwoman did not so much as bat an eyelid. She twisted to the side and threw up her arm, blocking the staff. *CRAAACK!*

Robin's staff flew into pieces. It was as if she was made of stone! The surprise attack didn't seem to hurt or faze Catwoman in the least! But Robin's brave move gave Batman a split-second advantage.

While Catwoman was distracted, Batman shoved her with as much force as he could summon. Catwoman skittered across the floor, crashing into a display of urns that shattered on the marble tile. *CRASH!*

Batman jumped to his feet. He used the distraction of the urns to move closer to Robin. Together they manoeuvred towards a door that led into the next room.

Catwoman's smile faded. She saw what Batman was up to. And she wasn't going to stand for it. The Dark Knight and his sidekick had freed themselves once. She wasn't about to let them slip away again.

Catwoman sprang onto the wall. She crawled straight up the vertical surface, clinging to it with her claws. Then, anchoring herself in the corner with one hand and two feet, she used her free hand to grasp her tail. Slowly she began to twirl it, picking up speed with each rotation. The lashing tail twirled faster and faster, slicing the air.

"Jump, Robin!" Batman commanded. Robin dived for the exit.

Catwoman flicked her wrist and sent her whip-tail flying. Using his ninja training, Robin tucked into a ball and rolled out of the room, narrowly avoiding Catwoman's tail.

KAH-RACK!

The slick black tail rebounded with a sound like thunder and shook the building. Batman's feline foe yowled in frustration. She did not like to miss. Growling, she began to swing her new weapon again. While the whip gained velocity, Batman tried to position himself so that he could escape the display room next.

Catwoman's eyes never left her foe, and she never stopped spinning her tail. She shoved off from her corner and landed on the other side of the room. Now clinging to the wall and ceiling in the opposite corner, she blocked Batman's retreat.

The Dark Knight could barely believe his eyes as he watched Catwoman jump from one wall to the other. Her strength was incredible! And Batman could tell by the look in her shady eyes, Catwoman was no longer playing. She wanted to claim the grand prize – Batman!

Slowly, Batman raised his hands, as if in surrender. Then, before Catwoman realized what he was doing, he threw his hands hard towards the floor. He had a little surprise for Catwoman. A smoke bomb that activated on impact flew from his fingers. It smashed into the ground and quickly filled the room with thick vapour.

FSSSSSSHHHH!

Cats might be able to see well in the dark with their special eyes, but they could not see through smoke.

As soon as the smoke bomb left his hand, Batman crouched down, changing his position. He heard the crack of Catwoman's whip lashing over his head, right in the spot where he'd last been standing. The mad cat meant business!

Batman activated the array hidden in the ears of his cowl. Using echolocation, Batman bounced high-frequency sound waves off the objects in the room. This allowed him to 'see' things the way that a bat would. He navigated easily out of the smoke while Catwoman flailed, blinded in the haze.

Moving silently, Batman took off through the exit and caught up to Robin. The Boy Wonder was holding his arm where it had been sliced by Catwoman's tail. Batman took Robin's uninjured arm and led him into another wing of the large museum.

The pair of heroes ran through the empty galleries as quietly as they could. At last Batman turned a corner and pulled Robin down behind a large sculpture. They were both breathing hard. Batman wanted to take a closer look at Robin's wound. And consider their options.

"You got away from her," Robin panted. Catwoman's startling transformation had him a little spooked! For a moment he had thought they were doomed.

Batman removed some first-aid supplies from his Utility Belt. He heard the relief in his partner's voice. Neither of them had ever seen anything like Catwoman's supernatural makeover – her strength, agility, whip-tail and razor-sharp claws . . . the threat the powered-up cat burglar possessed was very real. And the showdown wasn't over.

"I'm afraid getting away was the easy part," Batman said as he dressed Robin's wound. "The hard part will be making sure *she* doesn't get away from *us*."

Batman closed his eyes. He listened to the sounds of the museum at night. Even with the help of his high-tech sensory tools he could not detect any movement. He imagined that Catwoman was somewhere laying low, biding her time.

The Dark Knight concentrated, trying to imagine exactly what the feline mastermind was thinking. It was a sleuthing tool he often used to track down an opponent. By putting himself into a criminal's mind, Batman was usually able to predict the crook's next move. And Catwoman was a criminal he knew very well . . . at least before she had put on Atum-Ra's collar!

The precious choker had changed Catwoman in ways Batman never could have foreseen – making her stronger, angrier and much more deadly. Batman would not have believed the transformation if he hadn't witnessed it himself.

"Do you think she really has nine lives now?" Robin whispered.

It was a question Batman had been asking himself. If Catwoman possessed nine lives she would probably be willing to sacrifice one or more of them to escape . . .

CHAPTER 5

CAT FISHING

Batman accessed a blueprint of the Gotham City Art Museum in his heads-up display. His eyes flicked quickly back and forth as he scanned it.

"We have to build a better mousetrap," Batman murmured to himself.

Robin knew the Dark Knight was dreaming up something unique, something that would use Catwoman's own instincts and actions against her. But what were her weaknesses now that she had these new powers? Did any of them remain?

"We need to get that necklace off of her," Robin said. It was true. As long as Catwoman wore the necklace, she was unstoppable.

A slight change in Batman's breathing alerted Robin to the fact that his partner had hit on something. The Dark Knight suddenly switched off his display.

"You're right, Robin," he whispered. "And I think I know how."

***

Wordlessly, Batman led Robin to the sculpture garden. The outdoor courtyard had high walls. It was filled with statues and art pieces that ringed a central reflecting pool.

Working silently the duo dashed from one monument to the next. They repositioned the enormous sculptures and gathered a few objects from other parts of the museum.

"Now don't do anything foolish," Batman cautioned Robin.

"Oh, I won't," Robin reassured him. Then the pair split up.

Batman stayed behind to make sure the set-up was just right. Meanwhile, Robin slipped back through the museum corridor to find Catwoman and draw her out. The Boy Wonder listened carefully as he combed each wing of the museum.

After what felt like ages he finally caught sight of the thief. Silently, he watched her slinking through one of the galleries. She seemed half-mad and completely distracted by her new powers.

"Yoo-hoo . . . Batman!" she called, swinging her tail in lazy circles.

"Boy Wonder, where are yoouuuu?" she called. "Has the robin turned into a chicken?"

Robin's anger flared. He was no chicken! But he could not let her know that he was this close.

The Boy Wonder dashed back towards the sculpture garden and stopped short. He made a sharp turn and then tapped and dragged his fingers on the rough plaster wall.

TICHICK A CHICK A CHIC!

Robin made a noise that a cat could not resist. Then he waited a moment. He heard her footsteps. Catwoman had changed direction and was coming after him. *Perfect!*

Moving quietly Robin passed through a dark gallery filled with paintings and glass cases. When he got near the door he made another sound on purpose. He let his gloved hand scrape across the corner of a case. He knew Catwoman would want to pounce on that! He didn't know just how close she was!

From out of nowhere Catwoman appeared, flying through the air. She landed on Robin's cape, jerking him backwards. She glared up at him with yellow eyes, and flexed her huge claws.

"Gotcha!" she declared.

"Not for long," Robin shot back. He yanked his cape hard, upsetting Catwoman's balance. She scrambled, landing on her feet, of course. But the Boy Wonder was already sprinting away.

The young hero had completed the first part of his task – luring the cat to the trap. Now he needed to set up part two! As quickly as he could, Robin took his place. A high perch, out of harm's way . . . for now.

Before he could catch his breath, Robin spotted his pursuer on all fours at the entrance to the courtyard.

Catwoman slunk closer, looking more wild than ever. Her ears twitched. Her nose trembled. She tensed to attack. But to attack what? Which? Who? Her eyes darted here and there. The courtyard appeared to be full of Caped Crusaders!

A bit of fabric fluttered in one corner. A cape? Catwoman sprang at it, pinning a piece of harmless curtain to the floor.

MRRROOWR! She yowled in frustration.

Her head jerked up. She spied two dark points cast against the far wall. She propelled herself towards what she assumed was Batman's head with insane speed. All she caught were shadows and bits of masonry.

GRRRRRRRAAAWWWR!

"You think you're so clever!" she shouted into the dark. "But you can't hide for long."

On the edge of the courtyard wall Robin remained out of sight. Inside, Catwoman sprang from one hero decoy to another, shredding them with her claws and lashing them with her tail. She could not resist pouncing on every potential target!

There! And there! And there!

But each time she struck she came up with empty claws and cursed her enemies, hissing and spitting angrily.

When it grew quiet Robin knew that the moment they'd been waiting for was at hand. He peeked over the ledge of the wall.

Catwoman was opposite him, balanced on a tall sculpture. Below them, both could see an image of the Dark Knight, standing calmly in the courtyard, facing the other way. It would be easy for the super-charged villain to get to him in a single leap.

Catwoman recoiled, tensing every muscle in her body. Her tail curved, swishing back and forth.

Robin tensed too. He resisted the urge to call a warning to Batman. It looked like the end was near, but this was just what they had planned. Batman's image was the result of a double reflection.

The second that Catwoman pounced, Robin leaped too. He sped across the courtyard on a zip line they'd secured earlier. His timing was perfect. He intersected Catwoman's path in mid-air and snatched the Egyptian necklace from around her neck.

The effect was instantaneous. Robbed of her stolen powers, Catwoman plummeted towards the floor.

SPLASSSHH!

She landed in the central pool – right on top of Batman's image, which was being bounced from a carefully positioned mirror onto the water's surface.

Catwoman's claws and tail retracted. She instantly looked smaller when she was once again her normal self.

"Noooo!" Catwoman wailed, pounding and splashing the water.

Robin wasn't sure what she was angrier about, being fooled again or losing her god-like powers.

Batman silently stepped out of hiding and walked around the pool. He gazed at Catwoman hissing, spitting and dripping in the centre. She was angry with herself for being fooled by shadows and reflections – for being unable to control her impulses. It had cost her eight extra lives.

Suddenly the lights in the museum came on and police officers stepped into the sculpture garden. They had the two thugs from the front door in cuffs.

"Catwoman!" the police chief barked.

The drenched thief glared at the police chief and then turned her hard gaze on Batman. Cat and Bat locked eyes for a moment. Then Catwoman ran!

Using the sculpture closest to the edge of the wall, the black-clad thief catapulted herself upwards. When she reached the top, she paused for an instant to kick the enormous column-like statue over.

CRASH!

The round chiselled rock toppled but did not break. It rolled towards the Dynamic Duo, forcing them to leap for safety.

In the time it took to avoid being flattened, Catwoman was over the wall and gone. She did not have all of Atum-Ra's powers, but she still had a natural talent for disappearing into the dark night.

"She got away!" Robin cried. He couldn't believe they had lost Catwoman again.

"Yes, Robin. But we got what she came for," Batman said, indicating the relic still in Robin's hands.

Robin nodded as he handed the necklace to the police. It was true. They'd recovered the cat, the collar and now the ancient necklace. And he was exhausted from the long night of playing cat and mouse. But still . . .

"Think of it this way," Batman said, "tonight Catwoman escaped with one life, but we've got the other eight in the bag!"

CATWOMAN

REAL NAME: Selina Kyle

OCCUPATION: Professional thief

BASE: Gotham City

HEIGHT: 1.7 metres (5 feet 7 inches)

WEIGHT: 56 kilograms
         (125 pounds)

EYES: Green

HAIR: Black

Like Bruce Wayne, Selina Kyle was orphaned at a young age. But unlike Bruce, Selina had no guardians or family fortune to support her. Growing up alone on the mean streets of Gotham City, Selina was forced to resort to petty crime in order to survive. She soon became one of the city's most dangerous criminals. Becoming Catwoman to hide her true identity, Selina prowls the streets of Gotham City, preying on the wealthy while guarding Gotham City's fellow castaways.

- Selina's love of felines led her to choose a cat-related nickname. In fact, much of her stolen loot has been donated to cat-saving charities throughout the world.

- The athletic Selina prefers to use her feline grace and cat-like agility to evade her would-be captors. But when push comes to shove, Catwoman can use her retractable claws to keep her opponents at a distance.

- Selina has been an ally to Batman on several occasions. When a deadly plague spread through Gotham City, Catwoman teamed up with the Caped Crusader to help find a cure. However, their alliances never last, because Selina seems uninterested in putting an end to her thieving ways.

BIOGRAPHIES

Sarah Hines Stephens has been a children's book reader, editor, seller, buyer, author, copyeditor and ghostwriter for nearly 20 years – and she is still most of those things. She has published more than 100 books for children both original and licenced, and written about characters including Jedi, curious monkeys, super heroes, powerful princesses and disgruntled fowl. She lives in Oakland, California, USA, with her husband, two children and two dogs. When she is not doing book-related things, Sarah enjoys cooking, gardening, travelling, spending time with friends and family and dancing around in her kitchen.

Luciano Vecchio was born in 1982 and currently lives in Buenos Aires, Argentina. With experience in illustration, animation and comics, his works have been published in the UK, USA, Spain, France and Argentina. His credits include *Ben 10* (DC Comics), *Cruel Thing* (Norma), *Unseen Tribe* (Zuda Comics) and *Sentinels* (Drumfish Productions).

GLOSSARY

agility ability to move fast and easily

artefact object used in the past that was made by people

deity god or goddess

echolocation process of using sounds and echoes to locate objects; bats use echolocation to find food

enthusiast someone who is especially interested in a hobby or pastime

instinct behaviour that is natural rather than learned

myth false idea that many people believe

nocturnal active at night and resting during the day

pheromone smell produced by an animal

relic object that has survived from the past

sceptic person who questions things that other people believe in

velocity speed an object travels in a certain direction

DISCUSSION QUESTIONS

1. Robin tries to tell Batman about the necklace at the museum several times but gets interrupted. Would the Dynamic Duo have been able to foil Catwoman's plot sooner if the Boy Wonder had been allowed to explain?

2. In the story, Catwoman tries to steal precious jewellery and free the felines at the cat show. Which part of her plan was the most important to her? Explain why you think so.

3. Batman and Robin work together to stop Catwoman. Discuss a time when you worked with another person to solve a problem. How did working as a pair make it easier or harder to solve the problem?

WRITING PROMPTS

1. Catwoman grows more powerful when she puts on the necklace of Atum-Ra. Imagine if an article of your clothing could give you special powers. Write about your magical piece of clothing and describe what powers it would give you.

2. Robin taps his fingers and swishes his cape to lure Catwoman into the museum's courtyard. Think of another way the Boy Wonder could have got Catwoman's attention. Write a short scene in which Robin uses your idea and describe Catwoman's reaction to it.

3. At the end of the story, Catwoman escapes over the wall of the museum. Where does she go and what does she plan to do next? Write a short story that continues Catwoman's adventures.